SUSAN AND JAMES PATTERSON

Illustrated by
HSINPING PAN

Bigger WORDS for little geniuses

JIMMY Patterson Books
Little, Brown and Company
New York Boston London

Ailurophile (eye-LU-ruh-file)

Ailurophiles are folks who **adore** all kinds of cats and kittens. How *furry* sweet!

Bioluminescent
(bye-oh-loo-mih-NEH-sent)

Bioluminescent creatures have special **bodies** that light up in the dark.

Chasmophilous (kaz-MAH-fi-luhs)

Chasmophilous critters love to squeeze into nooks and **crannies** to hide.

Dolichopodous (dah-lih-KAH-puh-duhs)

Dolichopodous people have **delightfully** long feet...and big shoes!

Euneirophrenia (yoo-nay-roh-FREH-nee-ah)

After a dreamy dream, the peaceful and happy feeling you **enjoy** is called **euneirophrenia**.

Fünfundfünfzig (foon-foond-FOONF-zig)

Fünfundfünfzig is a **fun-fun-fun** word that means **fifty-five** in German!

Gnashnab (NASH-nab)

Don't be a **grouch**! A **grumbly** person who complains a lot can be called a **gnashnab**.

Hippopotomonstrosesquipedaliophobia

(hih-poh-PAH-toh-MON-stroh-sess-kwih-peh-DAY-lee-oh-FOH-bee-yah)

Hippopotomonstrosesquipedaliophobia is a **huge** word that means fear of big words!

Ichthyocoprolite
(ick-thee-oh-CAH-pruh-light)

Ichthyocoprolite is an **icky** word for fossilized fish poop from a long time ago.

Jabberwocky *(JA-buhr-wah-kee)*

Jabberwocky means nonsense, gibberish, mumbo **jumbo** and blah, blah, blah!

Knickknackatory (NICK-nak-kuh-TOH-ree)

A collection of beloved little trinkets you **keep** is called a **knickknackatory.**

Laterigrade (LA-tuhr-ih-grayd)

Most of us run forward, but **laterigrade** critters **love** to run sideways.

Melliferous (meh-LIH-fuh-ruhs)

Melliferous describes anything that helps **make** honey, like bees and flowers. How sweet!

Noctambulate *(nahk-TAM-byoo-layt)*

If you **noctambulate**, you are walking in your sleep at **night**.

Orchidaceous (or-kih-DAY-shuhs)

The word **orchidaceous** comes from **orchid** flowers, and it means you're a colorful dresser!

Papilionaceous
(puh-pih-lee-uh-NAY-shuhs)

Papilionaceous flowers look just like **pretty** butterflies.

Quaquaversal (kway-kwuh-VUHR-suhl)

A **quaquaversal** shape starts at the center and spreads out everywhere **quite** beautifully.

Rhinotillexomania
(RYE-noh-tuh-lex-oh-MAY-nee-ah)

A person with **rhinotillexomania** picks their nose **repeatedly**.

Somniloquent (sahm-NILL-oh-kwent)

Some people talk while they're **sleeping**. These chatterboxes are called **somniloquents**.

BLAH
BLAH
BLAH

Timbrophily (tim-BRAH-fill-lee)

Stamp collecting is **terrific** fun for people who have **timbrophily**.

Umbraculiform (uhm-BRACK-yoo-lih-form)

The word **umbraculiform** sounds like what it means—anything shaped like an **umbrella**.

Vulpecular (vuhl-PEH-kyuh-luhr)

Vulpecular is a **very** fancy way of describing something that reminds you of a fox.

Widdershins (WIH-duhr-shinz)

When you're **widdershins**, you're going counterclockwise or in the **wrong** direction.

Xertz (zerts)

Feeling really thirsty? Go ahead and **xertz**, or gulp down your drink!

Yoicks (yoyks)

Yoicks! That's a special word **you yell** to get **your** dog to chase other animals.

Zoanthropy (zoh-AN-thruh-pee)

A person with **zoanthropy** might believe they're an animal, like a lion, a monkey, or a **zebra**!

Here are more BIG WORDS for you to learn.

Abecedarian *(ay-bee-see-DAIR-ee-uhn)* — alphabetical order

Bibliophagist *(bih-blee-AH-fuh-jist)* — a person who loves to read books

Cynophile *(SIGH-noh-file)* — someone who adores dogs

Dendrophilous *(den-DRAH-fuh-luhs)* — when you are very fond of trees

Eellogofusciouhipoppokunurious *(ee-loh-goh-FOO-shee-oo-hih-POH-poh-koon-YOO-ree-uhs)* — very good

Friggatriskaidekaphobia *(frih-gah-TRISS-kie-deh-kuh-FOH-bee-yuh)* — the fear of Friday the thirteenth

Gallimaufry *(ga-lih-MAH-free)* — a mixed-up jumble of things

Hornswoggle *(HORN-swah-guhl)* — to fool someone

Imbroglio *(im-BROHL-yoh)* — a confusing situation

Jocoserious *(joh-koh-SEE-ree-uhs)* — mixing funny with serious

Kainotophobia *(kie-nah-tah-FOH-bee-yah)* — the fear of change

Lepidopterology *(leh-pih-dahp-tuhr-RAH-luh-jee)* — the study of butterflies and moths

Misodoctakleidist *(miss-oh-dock-tuh-KLIE-dist)* — a person who hates playing the piano

Nyctanthous *(nick-TAN-thuhs)* — describes plants with flowers that bloom at night

Which is the most fun word to say?

Ozostomia *(oh-zuh-STOH-mee-uh)* — bad breath

Psithurism *(SIH-thuhr-ih-zuhm)* — the sound of wind whispering through trees

Quinquagenarian *(kwin-kwuh-juh-NAIR-ee-yuhn)* — a person who is fifty years old

Rannygazoo *(ran-ee-guh-ZOO)* — a false story or foolish nonsense

Spectroheliokinematograph *(SPECK-troh-HEE-lee-oh-kih-nuh-MAH-tuh-graf)* — a special video camera that records the sun

Thalassophilous *(thah-luh-SAH-fih-luhs)* — having a love of the sea

Unzymotic *(un-zih-MAH-tick)* — fabulous

Vaccimulgence *(vack-sih-MUHL-juhnts)* — the act of milking cows

Whangam *(WANG-uhm)* — an imaginary animal

Xenodocheionology *(zeh-nuh-duh-kie-uh-NAH-luh-jee)* — the study of hotels and inns

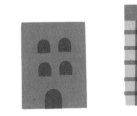

Yedda *(YEH-dah)* — a type of straw used for making hats

Zabaglione *(zah-buhl-YOH-nee)* — an Italian dessert of light custard

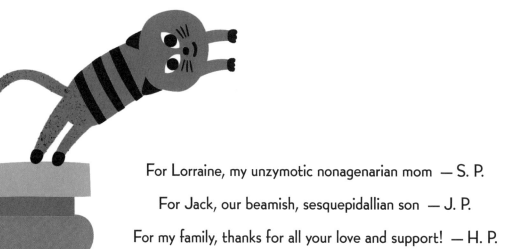

For Lorraine, my unzymotic nonagenarian mom — S. P.

For Jack, our beamish, sesquepidallian son — J. P.

For my family, thanks for all your love and support! — H. P.

ABOUT THIS BOOK

This book was edited by Jenny Bak and designed by Gail Doobinin with art direction by Tracy Shaw. The production was supervised by Lisa Ferris.

The text was set in Bernhard Gothic and illustrations were created using Adobe Illustrator and Photoshop.

Text copyright © 2019 by James Patterson and Susan Patterson / Illustrations copyright © 2019 by Hachette Book Group, Inc. / Illustrations by Hsinping Pan

Hachette Book Group supports the right to free expression and the value of copyright. The purpose of copyright is to encourage writers and artists to produce the creative works that enrich our culture. The scanning, uploading, and distribution of this book without permission is a theft of the authors' intellectual property. If you would like permission to use material from the book (other than for review purposes), please contact permissions@hbgusa.com. Thank you for your support of the authors' rights.

JIMMY Patterson Books / Little, Brown and Company / Hachette Book Group / 1290 Avenue of the Americas, New York, NY 10104 / jimmypatterson.org

First Edition: September 2019

JIMMY Patterson Books is an imprint of Little, Brown and Company, a division of Hachette Book Group, Inc. The Little, Brown name and logo are trademarks of Hachette Book Group, Inc. The JIMMY Patterson Books® name and logo are trademarks of JBP Business, LLC.

The publisher is not responsible for websites (or their content) that are not owned by the publisher.

The Hachette Speakers Bureau provides a wide range of authors for speaking events. To find out more, go to hachettespeakersbureau.com or call (866) 376-6591.

ISBN 978-0-316-53445-1 / LCCN 2019931564

10 9 8 7 6 5 4 3 2 1

IM / Printed in Italy